S/JP

P9-AFF-967

MARSHA WILSON CHALL

Sugarbush Spring

ILLUSTRATED BY JIM DALY

LOTHROP, LEE & SHEPARD BOOKS
New York

In the month of the Maple Sugar Moon, the snow's too wet for angel making, icicles rain from Grandpa's porch roof, and something is stirring in the woods. It's sugarbush spring.

Grandpa hitches Rosie and Jack to the cutter. My fingers peek out of my jacket—no mittens today—and Rosie nuzzles my hand for a treat. "Maple candy tomorrow," I promise her. She stomps and twitches and jingles her harness bells.

I wave to Grandpa, but he pulls me up next to him. "This year
you come with me," he says, then hands me the reins. "Rosie and
Jack know the way."

I bounce the reins on their rumps as light as Grandpa would.

"Sugar time, Rosie. Hee-yup, Jack," he calls.

Into the woods we slide, under branches that hold up the sky.
A crow puffs out his satin chest. *Caw...caw...caw.* The sun blinks
on tree-striped snow.

"Where's the sugar, Grandpa?"

"Inside the trees," he says. "Feeding them, helping them grow.
The trees give us their extra."

I find two holes in a maple, one on each side, like front and back belly buttons.

"Last year's taps," Grandpa tells me. "We'll open new ones this year."

Tap tap tap. There's one. *Tap tap tap.* Then the other. I hang a pail beneath each of them and wait. The sun side spills first. *Ping...ping...dripple, dripple-dripple.*

"She's running, Grandpa!" I shout.

Grandpa half fills a jelly jar with sap. "Spring tonic," he says, then sips and passes the jar to me.

I squint my eyes into microscopes. No bugs, no specks, ice clear. Mmmmm.

"Let's tap this one!" I shout, and try to reach around a trunk as wide as Rosie.

"Too old," says Grandpa. "See all the taps? She's given and given till she's nearly given out."

"How about this one?" I ask, wrapping my hands around another tree.

"Too young," Grandpa answers. "She needs all the sugar she makes this year. She'll be ready when she fills up your arms."

All around the sugarbush, I measure who is ready, filling up my arms with trees. We drill and tap and hang pail after pail until my feet are freezing and the *drip-drip-dripple* of a hundred trees has stopped.

"Grandpa, the trees are empty!" I shout.

Grandpa laughs. "They're just too cold," he tells me. "We'll have a freeze tonight. They'll rest up and run hard again tomorrow. Time to head back."

"Hee-yup, Rosie. Home, Jack," I call, and we slip through the purple woods under the Maple Sugar Moon.

When I wake the next morning, frost is melting on my window. I know that the trees are busy. The temperature is rising, the sap is running, the buckets are filling. And neighbors and friends have come to cook.

Grandpa gives us jobs. Mama and Dad drive Rosie and Jack through the sugarbush to gather the sap from our buckets. Donna Mae washes last year's syrup bottles. I polish them sparkly. Grandma makes chicken and dumplings to feed our hungry crew.

Molly and Ryan and I haul firewood into the sugarhouse. Daniel has built a monster fire to boil the sap. Jim will cook it down into thick syrup rivers.

The sugarhouse puffs out wet clouds as soft as fog. Ben and Ian leap through them and disappear.

"You're it!" Ryan tags Molly.

"Over here!" I shout. Molly chases me in and out of maple steam—bathtub warm, cotton-candy sweet.

Already the sugarhouse smells like pancakes.

"Is it syrup yet?" I ask Jim.

"Too soon," he says, and taps the thermometer. "Should be two hundred nineteen degrees. Seven degrees to go."

I keep my eye on that thermometer: two hundred fifteen…two hundred sixteen… The bubbles creep higher, swelling to the top of the pan. "There she blows!" I yell.

Jim flicks in a drop of cream, and the sap settles right back down, dark and gleaming. "A watched pot never boils over," he tells me.

The silver needle jumps—two hundred eighteen degrees. The sap boils into fine, golden bubbles…. Two hundred nineteen! Jim pours a caramel bubble from his long tin scoop. "We've got syrup!" he shouts.

Grandpa draws off the syrup, the first
two gallons, and filters it clean. "Too hot
to taste yet, but just right for sugar on
snow," he tells us. He drizzles the steaming
syrup on the snow, where it instantly
hardens, then trails it in ribbons for us to
pull and stretch and share with Rosie.
"Jack-wax," Grandpa calls it.

Around the cook fire, we eat dumplings, roast marshmallows, and tell stories while the cold sap flows into the pans, heats through, and thickens and boils. We stir and dip and skim till we draw off three more gallons.

But we're not done yet. "Two hundred more gallons of sap to cook before bed," Grandpa says. We toast our toes and take naps in chairs, in laps, or on dogs. Daisy doesn't mind. We pop corn and play checkers and Parcheesi way past our bedtimes until we've cooked the day's last batch. Ten gallons in all.

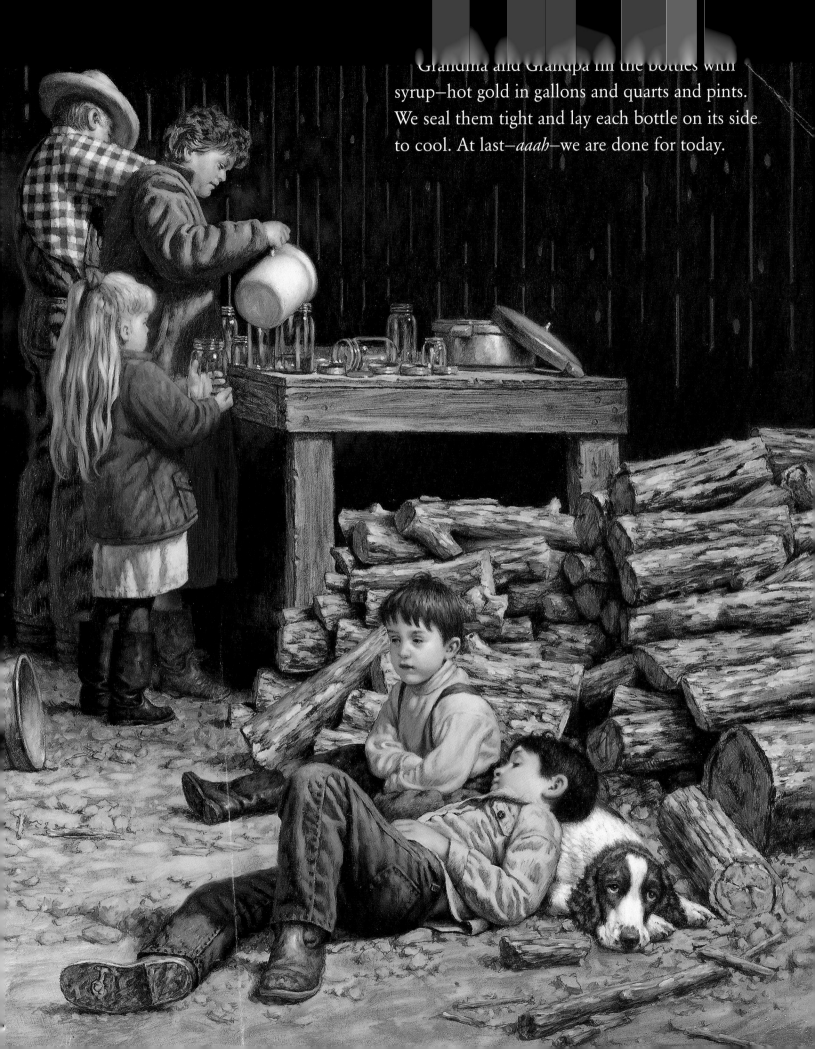

Grandma and Grandpa fill the bottles with syrup—hot gold in gallons and quarts and pints. We seal them tight and lay each bottle on its side to cool. At last—*aaah*—we are done for today.

Grandpa sets the first bottle in place on the windowsill next to the first bottle of last year's syrup and the first bottle of each year before that. Bottles colored like fall leaves—yellow and honey and bronze.

"A fine, light amber—Fancy Grade," Grandpa declares of this year's batch. There's room in the pantry for plenty more—enough for a whole year of pancakes, maple cream, and candy, then still some to sell. Enough till next year, when the woods stir and Grandpa and I again fill our arms with trees.

To my friends in the sugarbush,
especially the Flahertys of Maple Trails
and the Heaths
—MWC

To my wife, Carole,
for all the years of help and support
– JD

Oil paints on board were used for the full-color illustrations.
The text type is 14-point Garamond Regular.
Title calligraphy by Julian Waters
Text copyright © 2000 by Marsha Wilson Chall
Illustrations copyright © 2000 by Jim Daly
Published by Lothrop, Lee & Shepard Books
a division of William Morrow and Company, Inc.
1350 Avenue of the Americas, New York, NY 10019
www.williammorrow.com
Printed in Singapore at Tien Wah Press.
1 3 5 7 9 10 8 6 4 2
Library of Congress Cataloging-in-Publication Data
Chall, Marsha Wilson.
Sugarbush spring/by Marsha Chall; paintings by Jim Daly.
p. cm.
Summary: As winter melts into spring, a girl and her grandfather collect sap,
and then the whole family works through the night to make maple syrup.
ISBN 0-688-14907-3 (trade)–ISBN 0-688-14908-1 (library)
[1. Maple syrup–Fiction. 2. Family life–Fiction.] I. Daly, Jim, ill. II. Title. PZ7.C3496Su 2000
[E]–dc21 97-6458 CIP AC

A NOTE ON METRIC CONVERSIONS

Sap boils into syrup at 219° Fahrenheit, or about 104° Celsius. When Jim starts to watch the thermometer in this book, it measures 212°F, or 100°C. It must climb 7°F or 4°C before it becomes maple syrup. One gallon of syrup is equal to 3.785 liters of syrup.